To Grandpa Louie Metzger
— S.M.

Go to scholastic.com for web site information on Scholastic authors and illustrators.

Text copyright © 2001 by Scholastic Inc.
Illustrations copyright © 2001 by Hans Wilhelm, Inc.
All rights reserved. Published by Scholastic Inc.
SCHOLASTIC, CARTWHEEL BOOKS, DINOFOURS, and associated logos
are trademarks and/or registered trademarks of Scholastic Inc.

Library of Congress Cataloging-in-Publication Data

Metzger, Steve.
    Dinofours, it's Thanksgiving! / by Steve Metzger ; illustrated by Hans Wilhelm
        p. cm. — (Dinofours)
    "Cartwheel books."
    Summary: On the day before Thanksgiving, Brendan is angry because he cannot do anything that he wants and finds it difficult at school to think of anything for which he is thankful.
    ISBN: 0-439-29570-X
    [1. Behavior — Fiction. 2. Thanksgiving Day — Fiction. 3. Nursery schools — Fiction. 4. Schools — Fiction. 5. Dinosaurs — Fiction.] I. Title: It's Thanksgiving! II. Wilhelm, Hans, 1945- ill. III. Title.

PZ7.M56775 Dhv 2001
[E] — dc21

10 9 8 7 6 5 4 3 2 1

01 02 03 04 05

24

Printed in the U.S.A.
First printing, November 2001

DINOFOURS®
IT'S THANKSGIVING!

by Steve Metzger
Illustrated by Hans Wilhelm

Cartwheel
·B·O·O·K·S·®

SCHOLASTIC INC.
New York   Toronto   London   Auckland   Sydney
Mexico City   New Delhi   Hong Kong

"Let's go, sweetie," Brendan's mother said to Brendan. "It's time for school. Remember, Mrs. Dee said you'll be getting the classroom ready for tomorrow's Thanksgiving party."

"But I want to see the rest of my video," said Brendan. "It's my favorite one!"

"No, Brendan. We need to go," said Brendan's mother as she turned off the TV. "I don't want you to be late."

"You're a mean mommy," said Brendan. "I don't like you!"

Brendan's father bounded down the stairs.

"Brendan, please don't talk to your mother like that!" he said. "Now, let's go."

"But I want to see my video!" said Brendan.

Brendan's father took Brendan by the hand and quickly led him to the car.

Brendan sat quietly in the backseat. After a few minutes, he sang this song to himself:

My mommy is so mean.
My daddy's very bad.
If I could watch my video,
I wouldn't be so mad! Mad! MAD!

When they arrived at school, Mrs. Dee met them at the door. Before she could even say "hello," Brendan rushed right past her into the Dramatic Play area.

"What's going on with Brendan?" asked Mrs. Dee.

"Oh, he's just had a rough morning," Brendan's mother replied.

"He'll be fine," said Brendan's father.

"Bye-bye, Brendan," said Brendan's mother as she waved and walked outside with Brendan's father. "We're going to work now, but we'll see you later."

But Brendan didn't wave back. He went looking for the toy cash register instead.

At first, Brendan couldn't find the cash register, but then he saw Tara playing with it.

"Give me that cash register!" said Brendan as he tried to take it away.

"No!" said Tara, holding on tightly. "I had it first!"

Mrs. Dee came by to settle the problem.

"Brendan," said Mrs. Dee. "In a few minutes, *you* can have a turn with the cash register. In the meantime, I need you to help decorate the table for tomorrow's family Thanksgiving party."

"Oh, all right!" Brendan said. "But I *know* it won't be fun."

Brendan and Mrs. Dee walked over to the classroom area where three small tables were pushed together to make one giant party table. It was covered with taped-down pieces of large paper.

"Time to decorate," said Mrs. Dee. "You can use markers, crayons, or Thanksgiving stickers." Then she went to visit Albert in the blocks area.

"I'll use a brown marker," said Brendan. "I'm going to make the biggest turkey in the whole world!" He started to make a large circle with his marker.

"Hey!" said Joshua. "You're drawing on my stickers! Stop it!"

"But my turkey has to be big," said Brendan.

"Mrs. Dee!" Joshua called out.

"Brendan is drawing on my stickers!"

"Brendan, what's going on?" Mrs. Dee asked as she walked over.

"I'm making the biggest turkey in the whole world!" Brendan said. "See?"

"I see," said Mrs. Dee, "but can you make it just a little bit smaller so it doesn't touch Joshua's stickers?"

"No!" Brendan said, walking away. "I can't do *anything* I want to do. I'm having a terrible day!"

"I'm sorry to hear that," said Mrs. Dee, "but now it's Circle Time. Maybe that will cheer you up. Okay, everybody," announced Mrs. Dee in a loud voice, "it's time to gather on the rug."

The children sat down and looked up at Mrs. Dee.

"As you know," said Mrs. Dee, "tomorrow is our family Thanksgiving party for parents, grandparents, and baby-sit—"

"Yes," interrupted Tracy. "Tomorrow is our Thanksgiving party, and then Thursday, the day after that, is Thanksgiving! My big sister told me."

"That's right," said Mrs. Dee. "And today, because it's almost Thanksgiving, I'd like you to think of something that you are thankful for. It could be anything. I'll write down your words. Okay, Tara. Please begin."

"I'm thankful for my mommy and daddy," said Tara.

"I'm thankful for the sun and moon," said Joshua.

"I'm thankful for all my dolls and toys," said Danielle.

"I'm thankful for apples and chocolate cake," said Albert.

"I'm thankful for Mrs. Dee and my mommy
and my big sister," said Tracy.

Then it was Brendan's turn.
But he didn't say anything.

"Brendan," said Mrs. Dee. "What are you thankful for?"

"I'm not thankful for anything!" Brendan said as he stood up.

"I can't do anything I want to do — at home *or* at school!"

Then Brendan ran away from the Circle Time area.

Not watching where he was going, Brendan stepped on a toy car and fell flat on his back.

Mrs. Dee and the other children ran over to make sure he was all right.

Brendan was just about to yell and scream. But when he looked up, he saw the concerned faces of his friends and Mrs. Dee. Albert gently stroked his arm as Tara held his hand.

"Are you okay?" asked Mrs. Dee.

"Yes," said Brendan. "And now I *do* know what I'm thankful for."

"What's that?" asked Mrs. Dee.

"I'm thankful for having the best friends and teacher in the whole world," said Brendan.

The next day, the children's parents, grandparents, and baby-sitters all brought in special dishes for the Thanksgiving party. Everyone had a wonderful time eating, laughing, and telling stories.

Then, Brendan stood up and sang a new song:

I love my friends at school
And my teacher, Mrs. Dee.
I'm thankful for my mom and dad—
So thankful they love me.